FINN & BOTTS

TALENT SHOW TRICKS

FINN & BOTTS

TALENT SHOW TRICKS

STEW KNIGHT

Dreamwell Press

Copyright © 2019 Stewart Knight

Published by Dreamwell Press, Salt Lake City
www.finnandbotts.com

Edited and designed by Girl Friday Productions
www.girlfridayproductions.com

Editorial: Clete Smith, Amy Sullivan, Amy Snyder
Design: Paul Barrett
Illustrations: Mark Meyers

ISBN (Paperback): 978-1-7336092-2-7

First edition

Printed in the United States of America

For Sadie

CHAPTER ONE

Finn Fasser was not going to embarrass himself by being late today. He had worked too hard.

"Hustle!" Finn shouted to his best friend, Botts. Botts was running behind Finn, trying to catch up.

Finn dashed through the front doors of Mr. Labanzo's magic studio and looked up at the clock on the wall in the lobby. Three minutes to go before the start of the magic show. Finn had been practicing a difficult trick for today's performance, and Botts had agreed to help. He opened one of the double doors leading into a small auditorium and walked inside. The room was full of excited family members and friends facing the stage.

"So where are your mom and dad?" Liddy asked. She was standing near the doors, tying her hair into a ponytail. Liddy lived on Finn's street and was in the same third-grade classroom at Penn Wallow Elementary.

"They're both working today," Finn replied. "But they're coming to the talent show this week, so they won't miss anything." Finn went straight down the middle aisle and up onto the left side of the stage. After finding a place to leave his magic bag, he walked to the front row near some of the other magic students and sat down.

Botts stumbled into the studio tired, hot, and sweaty. And most of all—hungry. He felt like he had just finished a marathon, even though he and Finn had only run a few blocks to get here from the school. Finn motioned Botts to come sit by him.

Botts walked down the left side of the auditorium. He spotted Taz sitting on an aisle near the front row, eating a huge sandwich. Botts and Taz were two of the biggest students in the school and liked to tease each other. Botts quietly sneaked up behind Taz, grabbed the half-eaten sandwich from his hand, and stuffed it in his mouth.

"What's going on?" Taz said. He quickly looked up. Taz didn't know whether to yell or laugh. Botts's mouth was so full that his bulging cheeks looked as if they were going to explode.

"That's what happens when you wave a sandwich around like that," Botts said, barely able to speak. Grinning, Botts strolled to where Finn was sitting as if nothing had happened.

As Botts sat down, Finn heard someone sneering a few seats away on his right.

"The wannabe magician and his assistant have finally arrived. We can now start the show," said Felix, another student in Finn's third-grade class at school. Felix had been taking magic lessons from the Labanzo Magic Studio from the moment he could wave a wand and talk. He liked to remind Finn and every other student at school about what an amazing magician he was.

Finn started taking magic lessons from Mr. Labanzo just three months ago. He wanted to be in the upcoming school talent show and decided to perform a magic trick after watching the popular series *Tricks and Tips of the Top Magicians.*

Finn responded, "The best magic tricks are always worth—"

Suddenly, a group in the rear of the room yelled, "Go, Felix!"

Finn glanced back. The yelling was coming from Liddy and her friends in the back row. Liddy was Felix's magic assistant.

A door near the stage opened, and a large man entered. He was dressed in a black bow tie and tailcoat and had a white bushy mustache. Finn spun around and faced forward. The man stopped in the middle of the stage, looked down at the front row, and smiled.

"Thank you, parents, family members, and friends, for joining us today," the man said. "Welcome to the Labanzo Magic Studio. I'm Alfred Labanzo. Our performers have spent many hours practicing for the show today. Some of them will be performing in the school talent contest this week and have worked extra hard to prepare. For that reason, today's magic show should be extra thrilling. Now, let the show begin!"

Jenna, the newest magic student, performed the first act of the show. She walked onto the stage holding a black wand with white tips on each end. With three waves of the wand, a bright yellow flower instantly appeared from one end of the wand. The audience applauded.

Next was Bender. Bender announced that he would link two solid steel rings. He approached a young student in the third row and asked him to touch and feel the rings to confirm they were real. Bender returned to the stage and, to the amazement of everyone, not only linked and unlinked two rings but also added another ring and linked all three.

Following Bender, another magic student made a coin disappear in his hand and reappear in his shoe. One more followed with a rope trick.

It was then Felix's turn. Many in the audience were there to see him perform. Felix excelled at showmanship. He walked onto the stage with a mask over his eyes, a fake mustache, and a black cape with the letters *FF* embroidered in red on the back. Felix stepped next to a table covered with a black cloth and waved his wand. A banner unrolled from the table's edge. It read Felix Fantastico. Finn rolled his eyes. The back row cheered.

"Thank you, thank you," Felix said. "May I have a volunteer from the audience, please?"

Hands shot up. Felix pointed to Liddy, as expected. She got up from her chair and approached the stage.

Felix turned and smiled in Finn's direction, gleaming with confidence. Felix knew Finn was a better student in school than he was. But Felix wasn't going to let Finn become a better magician.

"Liddy," Felix asked. "Would you please examine each of the three colored boxes on the table?"

Liddy held up each box and looked inside.

"Is each box empty?"

"Yes," Liddy answered.

Felix reached into a bag on the floor and pulled out a plastic dove, a pretend mouse, and a fake flower. He displayed the items to the audience.

"As you can see, none of these are real," Felix said.

He then gave each of them to Liddy.

"Liddy will now place one item in each of the boxes."

After Liddy had finished, Felix grabbed his wand.

"I will now tap each box three times with my magic wand."

After tapping each box, Felix reached into each one and pulled out a real dove, a real mouse, and a real flower. The audience cheered. Felix bowed slowly.

"I will be performing at the school talent show this week," Felix said. "You won't want to miss my amazing trick or my amazing assistant."

Liddy turned a light shade of red as she walked off the stage. Felix removed his costume and returned to his seat.

Finn and Botts watched as Gemini walked onto the stage to perform.

Finn looked at Botts. "We're next."

Botts glanced back at Finn. "You're not getting all jittery on me, are you?" Botts asked.

Finn was already jittery. How was he going to match Felix's performance?

CHAPTER TWO

Gemini placed a stack of seemingly ordinary playing cards on the table and grabbed one from the top of the pile. When she slowly let go of the card, it floated in the air. The audience gasped. But Finn wasn't watching. His head was down as he went through each part of his magic trick. He wasn't going to make any mistakes today.

As Gemini returned to her seat, Finn and Botts stepped onto the stage. Botts arranged the props while Finn explained his trick.

"Ladies and gentlemen, my name is Finn, and this is my assistant, Botts. In a moment, I'll be chained to this chair with the four chains you see here on stage. The chains will be wrapped around my legs and arms and locked together with four locks. For each lock, there is a different key."

The audience was silent as they watched Botts demonstrate how each key fit each lock.

Finn continued, "After the locks are in place, each of the keys will be placed on the table in front of me, out of reach. I will then have thirty seconds to escape."

Finn sat down. His heart was pounding. He placed his arms on the armrests of the chair and pulled his legs tightly up against the chair legs.

Botts reached down and grabbed the chains. He wrapped a chain around each of Finn's legs and arms. Botts then fastened the chains together with the locks. Finn looked up at the audience and tried to appear calm.

"My assistant will now pull on the chains to make sure they're tight," Finn continued.

Botts pulled. There was no slack in any of them.

The audience remained quiet.

"I will now escape," Finn said in a dramatic voice. "Start the timer."

After pulling the black stage curtain in front of Finn, Botts walked over and pushed a button on the timer located on the table.

Immediately there was a voice from behind the curtain.

"Botts," Finn whispered.

Botts pulled the curtain back slightly.

Felix chuckled.

Botts looked at Finn with a puzzled face.

"What's wrong?" Botts whispered.

"I forgot something in my bag," Finn said in a low voice.

Botts ran offstage and, within a few seconds, returned with Finn's magic bag. As he stepped onto the stage, he tripped and fell. The students in the audience giggled. Embarrassed, Botts got up, walked over to the curtain, and slid behind it.

"What happened?" Finn asked.

"I tripped," Botts said, grinning. "At least we're not getting booed."

"Not yet," Finn said.

Botts held the bag just under Finn's right hand so Finn could reach inside. He then slipped back outside the curtain.

"We apologize for the delay," Botts said. He walked over and placed Finn's magic bag underneath the table. "Finn will now escape from his chains." Botts restarted the timer.

The sound of chains crashing to the ground came from inside the curtain as the timer reached thirty seconds. Botts pulled the curtain back. Finn was standing with three chains on the ground and one still partially wrapped around his ankle.

The audience clapped. Finn reluctantly bowed as he slipped out of the last chain and avoided looking at Felix. The curtain closed.

Botts pulled the chair, chains, and table back to the rear of the stage while Finn grabbed his bag and put the keys and locks inside. Mr. Labanzo returned to the stage.

"That concludes the first part of our magic show," Mr. Labanzo said. "I want to thank all of the students who performed so far. They all worked hard and did a great job. We will now take a ten-minute break to allow our next group to set up. Thank you."

"I'll take my bag," Finn said. "Can you bring the chains over to my house after the show?"

"And where are you going?" Botts asked. "Show's not done yet. You don't want to miss Cutter's magic-sword trick. He's going to put a sword through someone."

"I'm done," Finn said. He put his head down. "Tell me how it goes."

As he walked toward a side exit door near the stage, Finn heard the voice of someone he was hoping to avoid.

"Hey, Finn!" Felix shouted.

Finn turned his head in Felix's direction.

"I thought the highlight of the show was going to be Botts tripping," Felix said, laughing. "I was surprised to see it got better."

Without saying a word, Finn turned, then pushed open the door and walked out. He would never be as good as Felix.

CHAPTER THREE

Finn did not sleep well. He had spent most of the night thinking about his mistakes during the magic act. And when he walked into his classroom the next morning, the normal chattering of the students failed to distract him even a little from his gloomy thoughts about whether he was really cut out to be a magician. Ms. Twitchel, his teacher, had not yet arrived.

Finn noticed Botts was already in his seat near the front of the class. Botts had arrived earlier to do some makeup homework. Rather than say hi to Botts, he decided to just walk over and sit down in his seat next to Liddy.

"I liked the magic trick you did yesterday," she said, smiling.

"There's the great Houdini," Felix blurted. Felix was seated on the other side of Liddy. "Maybe Finn can help me with my next great trick."

Felix looked at Liddy, and then Finn, with a mysterious grin.

"My next trick will be simply watching my bad grades disappear," Felix said.

"How can you just change your grades without doing anything?" Liddy asked.

"Most people make their bad grades disappear by doing their homework," Tess interrupted. Tess was a friend of Finn's. She had overheard their conversation from her seat in the back of the classroom. "Maybe you could do a little abracadabra on yourself, Felix," she continued, "and go from lifeless to lively and actually do something to get good grades. Give that a try first, you magical goofball."

"Getting a little lonely in the rear of the classroom?" Felix snapped back. "Maybe you could play some one-finger nursery-rhyme songs for us on the piano—the ones that you're working on for the talent show."

"Back off, you two," Liddy said. "Listen, Felix, why don't we just get a study group together?"

"And invite the *smartest* guy in the class," Felix added. "What do you think of that, genius?" Felix continued as he looked back at Finn. "Not a bad idea. But Finn has another skill we can use."

Felix had a deviant smile on his face as he continued to stare at Finn. Finn avoided his glare and looked up at the clock. Just three minutes to go before school started. Finn usually wanted school to end, but this was the first time he could think of when he wanted it to start. The last thing Finn needed was for Felix to say something more about his botched magic act the day before at Labanzo's studio.

"So, Finn, here's a chance to show your stuff," Felix said, smirking. "You're good at imitating voices."

"It's true," Liddy said, glancing over at Finn. "I remember you imitating some of your neighbors at your sister's birthday party last summer."

"He does a great impression of the principal," Botts said, joining in.

Finn looked over at Botts and silently mouthed the words *Shut up.*

"Class!" Felix yelled out. "Finn is going to imitate whiny Mr. Beaker. I know he can do it. And to make it even more fun, Finn is going to call clueless Ms. Flappet on the school intercom system and tell her—as Mr. Beaker— that all the students from Ms. Twitchel's class will receive As in science." Mr. Beaker was one of the science teachers at Penn Wallow and Ms. Flappet was the principal's assistant.

"What do you say, Houdini?" Felix teased as he turned toward Finn.

Finn was shocked. Not at what he had just been asked to do, but that Felix had the nerve to tell the rest of the class that he was going to do it. And even if he did do it, what if Ms. Flappet asked for something only Mr. Beaker would know? He wouldn't know what to say and would probably end up being caught.

"Sorry," Finn said. "Not going to do that."

"It's just Flappet," Felix responded. "Even if Mr. Beaker finds out, he'll think Flappet was hearing voices or made the grade changes by mistake."

"It would be pretty funny," Taz said.

Liddy just looked over, smiled, and shrugged her shoulders.

"You can do it," Felix said. "You're the best!"

Rather than ignoring them, pressure began to build inside Finn to do it. Did he want to impress everyone—or just make up for his poor magic performance yesterday? He couldn't believe he was even thinking about it.

Some of the students chanted, "Do it! Do it!"

Finn looked around and, with a deep breath, got up and went over to the intercom button on the wall near the door. *After all,* he thought, *Flappet is harmless.* If her hearing is as bad as her eyesight, anyone could do this.

Everyone looked at Finn. Finn looked up at the clock again. One minute to go before the starting bell rang. If he was going to do his impression of Mr. Beaker, it was now or never. Finn pushed the intercom button.

"Ms. Flappet," Finn said, his voice high-pitched and whiny. "This is Mr. Beaker."

"What can I do for you, Mr. Beaker?" she replied.

Finn's voice was a near-perfect match to Mr. Beaker's. All the students were struggling not to laugh out loud.

"I just wanted to let you know that because the students in Ms. Twitchel's class have done so well on their science tests and assignments, I've decided to give them all As this quarter," Finn said. "Can you make those changes on the school computer for me?"

"Why, certainly, Mr. Beaker," Ms. Flappet said. "But I'll need you to come to the office and sign the student grade-change forms."

"No problem," Finn said. "Thanks." Finn released the intercom button.

Everyone in the class roared with laughter except Tess. Finn felt a flash of empty acceptance. But that feeling stopped as Ms. Twitchel walked into the classroom.

"Finn," she said in a stern voice, "can you come here?"

Finn walked into the hallway. Mr. Beaker was standing right next to her. Finn felt certain he was going to be suspended from school for the first time in his life.

"I'm disappointed, Finn," said Ms. Twitchel. "That's definitely not your style. And unfortunately, I have no choice but to put you in lunch detention today. And during lunch detention, you'll have an opportunity to write Mr. Beaker an apology letter."

Finn looked over at Mr. Beaker. He was not smiling. Finn sighed.

"Back to your seat, Finn," Ms. Twitchel said.

Ms. Twitchel returned to the front of the classroom.

"Class," Ms. Twitchel said, "time to settle down and begin. Math books out."

Finn sat down. He was stunned. What did he just do?

Liddy looked over at him and whispered, "I'm sorry, but you really were amazing."

Felix overheard. He waited for Ms. Twitchel to turn her back to the class to write down the assigned math problems on the board.

He then leaned toward Liddy.

"Don't worry about Finn," Felix said. "He'll be fine. Just remember—I'll have straight As before the end of the week in all my classes. And the entire school will be amazed."

CHAPTER FOUR

The bell rang for lunch. Ms. Twitchel handed Finn his detention notice with instructions for Ms. Flappet. Finn avoided eye contact with anyone as he walked down the hall. When he entered the main office, he walked over to Ms. Flappet seated at her desk. After reading the notice, she looked up with a curious smile.

"Mr. Beaker is such a nice teacher," Ms. Flappet said. "I didn't think anyone could make him upset—especially you. Why did Ms. Twitchel ask you to write an apology letter?"

"I pretended to be Mr. Beaker and asked for some student grades to be changed," Finn replied.

"I find that hard to believe," she said. "I heard Mr. Beaker on the intercom this morning. And it certainly didn't sound like you."

Finn managed a small smile. He thought he would confuse Ms. Flappet if he tried to explain.

"So where do I go?" Finn asked unhappily. He quickly glanced around the busy main office for other unhappy students who would be joining him.

"You just missed it," she said, pointing. "Go right across the hall. You'll see a room with a sign on the door that says Detention. Try to finish your letter to Mr. Beaker today. One of the students has been in lunch detention for three days. He's working on an apology letter for putting dog food in student lunches. Trust me—you don't want to be back here tomorrow."

Finn walked out of the main office and into the detention room. The single window looked out into the hallway and the main office. Ms. Olive, a student teacher, was sitting at a desk in front of the class. She handed him the sign-in sheet without looking up.

"Can I see your detention notice?" Ms. Olive asked. She skimmed it and handed him a pen and paper. "Your seat for the next thirty-five minutes will be next to Bellow on the left. And no talking."

"I guess even the good kids need to do some time," Bellow whispered, trying not to laugh as Finn sat down.

"No talking includes you, Bellow," Ms. Olive said. "I have no problem adding an extra day of detention for you. But I don't think you want to come back for day four."

Bellow must have been the one Ms. Flappet was talking about. Finn wasn't surprised. Bellow was the school bully and teased everyone.

Finn looked down at the empty piece of paper. He wanted to tell Mr. Beaker he was pressured and that it wasn't really his fault. But Mr. Beaker wouldn't believe him. And besides—it really was his fault. And his mom would be reminding him as well, after Flappet called her tonight to report his detention.

Finn began to write. He thought about how Felix had talked him into pretending to be Mr. Beaker. He thought about how he messed up on his magic trick at Labanzo's studio. As his mind drifted, he looked out into the hall. Through the crowds of passing students, he could see the list of performers for the talent show. It was on the electronic events screen just outside the main office in the hallway. The list would scroll up until all the names had been displayed and then start over again. Finn counted. There were at least twenty students who had signed up. He recognized most of the names.

Tess was playing the piano, Veronica was singing, and, of course, his sister, Selina, and Botts's sister, Tara, were dancing. Botts and Taz were both riding unicycles in separate performances. Ringo was playing the drums with his band. And at the end was Felix.

Finn looked up at the clock. He now had three minutes before lunch ended. He wrote his last sentence and signed his name. After reading through the finished letter, he counted three places where he had apologized. Mr. Labanzo always said the number three is a magician's friend. He remembered the phrases Labanzo used like *Third time's the charm* and *Count to three when tapping your wand.* Maybe

Mr. Beaker would forget this whole mess after reading the letter or at least say something nice to his parents when they came for parent-teacher conference next week.

The ending lunch bell rang. He gave the letter to Ms. Olive and opened the detention-room door. Botts and Tess were waiting for him by the events screen across the hall.

"Deedee has trained her parakeet to pop bubble-gum bubbles," Botts said. "That's going to be funny."

"Do you think Principal Biggs is going to let Yang and Zhang use real swords as part of their kung fu performance?" Tess asked.

"All I know," Finn said, "is that I'm standing next to the best piano player and unicycle rider in the school. Are you both ready?"

Tess and Botts ignored him and read the entire list as it scrolled down.

"Did you notice who's missing from this list?" Tess asked.

"Who?" Finn replied.

"You," Botts answered. "There's no way we're going to let Felix be the only magic act."

Botts began to walk into the office to request that Finn's name be added to the talent show.

"Stop!" Finn said. He grabbed Botts by the arm. "I took my name off the list. I made myself look dumb at Labanzo's yesterday. And now I have a lunch-detention notice. I just can't do it. Besides, I'm helping Selina and Tara with their dance performance. That's good enough for me."

Finn went silent for a moment. "I don't want to embarrass myself anymore," he said. Before Botts or Tess could respond, Finn turned and walked back to the classroom.

CHAPTER FIVE

After school, Finn walked to Botts's house for the final dance rehearsal. Tara and Selina had changed Tara's garage into a temporary dance studio. A thin carpet covered the floor. A small sound system and some speakers sat on a table in the corner. Next to the table stood a big spotlight mounted on a stand. Two other dancers, Elle and Willow, were also there for the rehearsal.

"Did you decide to be in the magic show?" Selina asked.

"No plans," Finn replied. "Just trying not to embarrass myself anymore."

"Well, we're happy to have your help," Tara responded with a smile.

Selina gave Finn a detailed list of lighting cues on when and where the spotlight would be used during the dance performance. At the school auditorium, the stage crew would be controlling the rest of the lighting.

"Let's get started!" Selina shouted. Selina looked over at Finn. "After we go through it, you'll feel more comfortable with how the spotlight works."

Selina and the rest of the group got into their starting positions: two in front and two in back, with a chair in the middle as part of the performance.

Finn started the music. He followed the cues as the music progressed, shining the spotlight on each dancer at the right time. After rehearsing the dance for the third time, Mrs. Buttons, Botts's mom, opened the kitchen door leading into the garage and looked over at Finn.

"Finn," she called out, "someone wants to talk to you outside."

Finn walked through the kitchen and out the front door. Mr. Labanzo was standing in the driveway.

"Mr. Labanzo," Finn said with surprise. "What are you doing here?"

"Sorry to interrupt," Mr. Labanzo replied. "But someone told me you've decided not to be in the show." He looked sad.

Finn stood silently and looked at the ground. He didn't want to make Mr. Labanzo feel any worse by telling him about his time in lunch detention today.

"I hope your performance yesterday at the studio is not stopping you," Mr. Labanzo said.

"When I was a young magician, my first trick was to make a coin disappear using sleight of hand. I practiced for many hours. But until I believed I could make that coin disappear, I couldn't master the trick."

Finn now looked up at Mr. Labanzo.

"Your audience will believe in you if you believe in yourself," Mr. Labanzo continued. "I have only one student who can perform the unbreakable-chain trick. That's you. Even Felix hasn't taken the time to practice it. I've told Felix I'll be at the talent show. And I wanted to tell you as well. I'm hoping to see both of you perform."

Without saying another word, Mr. Labanzo turned, walked back to his car, and got in. He waved his hand, as if he had just finished the last trick of a magic show, and disappeared from view.

CHAPTER SIX

The next morning on their way to class, Finn and Botts stopped to read the huge banner over the main entrance to the auditorium.

Penn Wallow School
Talent Show
1:00 Today

"You know, you still have time," Botts said.

"Next year," Finn replied. "Everyone will have forgotten by then."

Botts chuckled. "Not Felix, he—"

"Hey, Botts," Taz interrupted as he and Felix walked past. "I was wondering if I could ride your tricycle after the show?"

Taz and Felix both laughed. Finn turned to Botts with a puzzled look.

"That's what the talent-show list says," Felix added. He smiled and shrugged.

Finn and Botts turned and ran back down the hall toward the main office. Tess was looking at the screen when they got there.

"Someone's made changes to the talent-show list," Tess said.

Finn and Botts started reading. Tess would be playing the piano with her toes. Veronica would be humming a kazoo. Tiny would be balancing on her tongue. Deedee's parakeet would be picking her nose. And Botts would be riding a tricycle. Tess walked into the main office before Finn and Botts finished reading all the changes.

Within a minute, Principal Biggs came out with Tess behind him. He walked over to the screen and read through the descriptions of each talent-show act. After finishing, he turned and looked at each of them. "I'll find out who did this," he said firmly. "Thank you for letting me know. Please return to class. The first bell is about to ring, and I don't want any of you to be late."

• • •

The morning seemed to go on forever. Finn was hoping for something to interrupt his science and math assignments he had been working on for over an hour. Finally, at 12:30 p.m., Principal Biggs's voice came on over the school intercom system.

"Students and teachers," Principal Biggs announced. "The talent show will start at one o'clock. Talent-show participants are now excused to go to the auditorium to prepare for the show. All other students may be excused at 12:45. Thank you."

Ms. Twitchel made her own announcement. "Those who are participating in today's talent show may leave, but only after your desks are cleaned up."

Finn, Botts, and Tess hurried to pack up their books and headed out the classroom door. Felix was close behind them when they reached the auditorium.

Botts and Tess went down a side hall and through a rear door. Finn walked into the auditorium using the main doors.

Finn grabbed the spotlight and its stand in the rear corner of the auditorium and carried them to the platform in the middle section of the seats. Selina had told him that morning where she would put them. Finn attached the stand to the spotlight.

Selina also wanted him to rehearse the lighting for their dance with the stage crew. The stage lighting was operated from the control booth in the rear of the auditorium. Finn hurried back to the control booth to tell the stage crew he was ready. As he reached for the door, he heard an unexpected voice.

"Finn, stop!" Felix shouted. Felix walked toward him, his right arm holding his stomach while coughing into his left arm. Felix's face was tense. Finn stopped and waited. Felix looked around to make sure no one could hear him.

"There is no way I can do my act," Felix said quietly. "I'm really sick. And since you're not in the talent show, I thought you might want to take my place?"

Finn looked carefully at Felix to see if he was looking for one more opportunity to embarrass him.

"You're joking, right?" Finn asked.

"I'm serious," Felix replied. "You can wear my mask and cape and everything else. You're about my size. But you just can't tell anyone it was *you* on stage."

Strange request, Finn thought. But if he made a mistake again, it would be Felix making the mistake. And if he succeeded, he would prove to himself he could do it. Finn didn't care if no one knew he would be the one performing.

"Yes, on one condition," Finn blurted.

"Great, what is it?" Felix asked.

"I get to decide which trick I perform," Finn replied.

"Deal," Felix said. "My magic-trick props are backstage. And my costume is in a black-and-red bag in the dressing room. Can't miss it. Thanks."

As Felix walked away holding his stomach, Finn picked up a program from an adult volunteer and raced down the aisle to the front stage. Felix was the last talent act on the program. He motioned to Botts to come down from the stage. Botts got off his unicycle and shuffled down the stage stairs.

"You're cutting into the practice time of the next talent-show winner," Botts said.

"Listen," Finn responded. "Your sister and Selina are getting their dance equipment and clothes from your mom's car right now in the front parking lot. Can you run outside and ask your mom if she can go to my house, grab my magic bag, and bring it to school? I need to go right now and rehearse the lighting with the stage crew for their dance."

"Why do you need your magic stuff?" Botts asked. "You're not in the talent show."

"I'll explain later," Finn replied as the bell rang, excusing the students for the talent show.

CHAPTER SEVEN

Botts hustled out of the auditorium and through the main school doors to the front parking lot. Finn went up the stairs to the control booth. Gator was busy adjusting the stage lights using a large lighting console. Gator was the student stage-crew director. He was a fifth-grader. Bedford, another member of the stage crew, was doing sound checks.

Finn walked over to Gator and handed him an envelope. "Here are the lighting directions and music for Selina and Tara's performance," Finn said.

"Then I'm ready to rehearse!" Gator exclaimed. "We have about ten minutes before the show starts. Here's a headset for you. I can play the music through the headset so we can practice while you're down at the spotlight."

Finn returned to the platform. He climbed up and turned on the spotlight, then adjusted his headset and spoke into the tiny microphone. "Ready," Finn said.

"OK," Gator said. "Starting in three, two, one—begin!"

The song played through his headset, and Finn followed the cues. Gator controlled the timing of all the stage lights overhead so they would turn on and off with the beat of the music. Finn moved the spotlight back and forth to the correct locations and turned it on and off at the right times, just like he had done at the rehearsal in Tara's garage. Selina waved to Finn as she and Tara walked onto the stage with their equipment.

Gator's voice came on through the headset after the music ended. "Great job on the spotlight. Nice blend with the stage lighting. We're ready. You keep the headset, and when we get to Selina and Tara in the program, I'll call you. Talk to you later."

Finn looked at the clock as he walked out the auditorium doors to find Botts. Three minutes to go before the start of the talent show.

Botts entered the front doors of the school holding Finn's bag. Mrs. Buttons waved from her car as she drove away.

"How's that for timing?" Botts said, gasping. He handed Finn his bag.

"You're not done," Finn said with a smile.

"You're asking me to work *overtime* now?" Botts questioned. "Finn, I've missed out on

some valuable practice time because of you. You owe me—big time."

"I'll make it up to you," Finn replied.

Finn then became serious. "Listen—if I go backstage right now with this bag, everyone will ask me what I'm doing. So please take the bag and put it in the dressing room next to Felix's costume bag. The one with the letters *FF* on it."

"All right, all right, I'll find Mr. Fantastico's bag," Botts said. "And I won't ask any questions—right now. And even if I wanted to ask, I won't. You and I have less than one minute to go before the talent show starts."

"Thanks, Botts," Finn said.

Finn watched Botts as he raced down the side hall to the rear entrance of the auditorium. Just inside were the dressing rooms. For a moment, Finn wondered if Felix had tricked him. He waited, looking down the hallway, expecting Botts to come lumbering back to tell him that Felix was wearing his costume and rehearsing with Liddy. But there had been no sign of Felix since they last talked. And Liddy was sitting with her friends in the front of the auditorium.

Finn hurried back, then opened the auditorium doors and walked inside. The lights dimmed as he reached his seat near the spotlight platform.

He felt a chill go through his body as he realized he would be performing in front of the entire school. But this time, he would perform at his own pace and in his own way, without anyone knowing. He began to rehearse the chain trick in his mind, just as he had done prior to his performance at Labanzo's studio. The nervousness inside him vanished. *This will be my best performance,* he told himself. There was no turning back.

CHAPTER EIGHT

With the auditorium now dark except for the aisle lights, Principal Biggs walked onto the stage. There was standing room only.

"Welcome!" Principal Biggs exclaimed. "I look forward to the talent show each year. I'm excited to see so many exceptional students performing this afternoon. We will proceed in the order shown on your program. Let's get started!"

The curtain lifted. Seated at the piano was Tess. She started at the top of the keyboard and played to the bottom and back. She moved so quickly that her fingers were just one big blur. After she finished her piece, the entire audience stood up, clapping and cheering.

Veronica was next and sang a hit Broadway song. Her voice was so high and loud that one of the parents near Finn started to whisper about the lights breaking.

Tiny followed. She amazed everyone by holding herself up with a one-arm handstand. From that moment on, no one challenged Tiny in an arm-wrestling contest.

Finn glanced back down at the program. One student would be playing the violin, and another student would be performing yo-yo tricks. Selina and Tara's dance group would perform after that.

After the violin performance, Bedford alerted Finn on his headset that he was ready in the control booth. Finn climbed onto the platform and stood behind the spotlight. He

called back to say he was in position. Following the yo-yo act, Selina, Tara, Elle, and Willow walked onto the stage and took their places. The music started. But no one moved. Finn spoke into his headset.

"That's the wrong music," Finn whispered.

"Sorry," Bedford said. "Gator was supposed to label the music. We thought we had the right one. But Gator isn't here."

Finn repeated the music title and confirmed they had the written cues for the lighting.

"OK, we found it," Bedford said.

Finn gave Selina and Tara a thumbs-up. The correct music started, and the dance performance began. As the stage lights changed colors, Finn moved the spotlight. He watched as the dancers followed their routine perfectly. When the dance finished, the audience cheered. Finn hoped Selina was happy. It was hard hiding from her when she was angry

Finn turned off the spotlight, climbed down from the platform, and returned to his seat.

Taz was next. But no one could find him. The last time Finn had seen him was with Felix. Finn knew Taz had practiced hard for the talent show. He sensed something wasn't right.

The program continued. Yang and Zhang seemed to hover in the air with their high jumps and kicks during their kung fu routine. Finn was impressed with both of them—even without their swords. Principal Biggs had seen both of them practicing with the swords backstage before the show started and had taken them away.

More students followed. Lulu performed a funny tap dance, another student played the harp, one spun three large hoops around her body, and another used a pogo stick a~ jump rope at the same time. After b~

four cups on his head for ten seconds, Oscar stumbled but managed to catch all the cups with his hands when they fell.

Botts was next. All the students liked Botts's playful nature, and watching him try to balance on a unicycle, as one of the biggest students, was funny. Seeing him actually ride was impressive. The cheering from the audience started immediately as he rode up and down three angled ramps placed in a circle. Two tall tables were in the middle. A plate stacked with chocolate donuts was on top of each table. After three times around the ramps, Botts stopped his unicycle at a table. He picked up a plate and ate a donut. He balanced the plate with the rest of the donuts on his head and began to pedal.

Within one minute, Taz entered the stage from the back on his unicycle and picked up the other plate with chocolate donuts on it.

Botts then pedaled furiously after Taz around the ramps. Both were screaming at each other as they went up and down in circles. When Botts caught up with Taz, Taz hurled donuts at Botts. Botts, now covered with chocolate donuts, hurled donuts back. He then lunged at Taz. The audience became hysterical as both came crashing down onto the stage floor. The curtain dropped.

From his seat, Finn could see Botts was angry. Finn couldn't recall Botts saying anything about Taz being part of his act. Why would Taz miss his turn on the program and show up now? Something was definitely wrong.

CHAPTER NINE

Finn felt a tingling sensation travel through his body. There were only five performers left before it was his turn. As the stage crew removed the ramps and cleaned up the mess left by Botts and Taz, he quietly got up from his seat and left the auditorium. There were so many people in the backstage area that no one noticed him as he slipped into the dressing room.

Finn found his bag next to Felix's in the third stall and closed the door. As he put on Felix's costume, he could hear Ringo performing his drum solo onstage with the rest of his rock band. By the time Ringo and his band finished playing, Felix's cape was around Finn's neck, the mask was over his eyes, and the fake mustache was stuck under his nose.

He walked out of the stall with his magic bag and faced one of the mirrors. *Not bad,* he thought. He listened to the song Penny was lip-synching as he adjusted the cape and left the dressing room. The stage crew and other performers walked past him without saying a word. He breathed a sigh of relief that no one had recognized him. He knew he could pass as Felix's twin from a distance. But up close, there was no resemblance except for the costume.

Another student was playing the guitar as he walked to the backstage area to find the chair Tara had used for the dance performance. He moved just behind one of the backstage curtains, where he could see the remaining two performers: Boxster and Deedee.

Boxster played a medley of polka music as a one-person band. His crazy collection of instruments included an accordion, a harmonica around his neck, and a bass drum mounted on his back with a set of cymbals on top that he could operate with a foot pedal.

Deedee walked out with her trained parakeet on her shoulder. As soon as she finished blowing a big bubble, the parakeet instantly leaned over and popped it, covering Deedee's face with pink gum. The audience laughed, and the curtain dropped.

Finn directed the stage crew on where to place the chair and the rest of his equipment. He also explained that the magic boxes—containing the fake dove, mouse, and flower—would not be used. Luckily, the stage-crew members were older students, and none of them recognized him.

He took a deep breath and walked onto the middle of the stage. Some of the students started chanting, "Felix! Felix! Felix!" Finn smiled with confidence. He was ready. Felix would not be performing his magic-box trick today. He would be performing the unbreakable-chain trick. And it would be flawless. Finn signaled for the curtain to go up.

CHAPTER TEN

Music blared from the auditorium speakers in unison with a dazzling light display. Clearly, Felix had worked out a grand start to his performance with the control-booth crew. Finn walked over to the chair. Four chains were draped over it.

"Ladies—" Finn started and then stopped. He may look like Felix from a distance, but he didn't sound like Felix. Finn had forgotten about their voices being different. His mind began to race for a solution. If he could imitate

Mr. Beaker's voice without practicing, he could imitate Felix.

Remembering the sound and speech pattern of Felix's voice, he continued, "And gentlemen. I will now attempt to escape from this chair after being fastened to it with these four solid-steel chains and locks. And I will do it blindfolded."

Finn decided to add the blindfold after seeing it in Felix's bag. Labanzo had shown him how to use it with any trick. This was his opportunity.

"May I have an assistant from the audience?" Finn shouted, using his Felix voice.

As planned by Felix, Finn looked and pointed to Liddy. She got up from her seat and walked up to the stage. As he waited, Finn noticed light coming through one of the rear auditorium doors as it opened. It was Mr. Labanzo.

"Liddy will now pull on the locks and chains to show they are real," Finn said.

Liddy looked at Finn strangely.

"Why are we doing this trick?" Liddy whispered. She turned away from the audience. "I thought we rehearsed the magic boxes."

"Changed my mind," Finn said.

She picked up the chains and locks.

"I'm not sure I can remember this," Liddy said in a low voice.

"You can do it," Finn said. He turned toward her. "Just listen to me."

She smiled and faced the audience.

"Are you feeling OK, Felix?" Liddy said. She was now trying to speak without moving her lips. "You don't sound like yourself."

Finn quickly turned his back toward the audience and looked directly at her. "Zip it," he whispered. "I'm fine. But if you keep talking, the audience will think something is not fine."

Still smiling, Liddy pulled and strained on the four chains and locks to show the audience they were real. Finn turned around and sat down in the chair. The audience was completely still—except for Ringo, who had decided to do a drumroll behind the stage.

"Liddy will now wrap each of the four chains around my arms and legs and fasten them to the chair with the locks," Finn announced. "And for each lock, there is a different key. Liddy will demonstrate."

The audience was silent as they watched Liddy open each lock with one of the four keys. After opening the locks, she placed the keys on top of the table in front of the stage and returned.

With Finn's direction, Liddy chained Finn's wrists and ankles to the arms and legs of the chair and locked each of the chains.

"And now the blindfold," Finn requested.

Liddy picked up the black blindfold and tied it around Finn's head. The dramatic music continued to play throughout the auditorium, along with Ringo's drumming.

"Ladies and gentlemen," Finn said. "After Liddy pulls the curtain in front of me, I will attempt my escape. And I will do it in less than thirty seconds. Start the timer."

Liddy pulled the curtain and pressed the timer's start button. She led the audience in a countdown after the timer reached ten. When the timer reached zero, Liddy pulled back the curtain. Finn was standing beside the chair. The chains and locks were on the ground. The parents and students in the audience stood up and cheered. Finn bowed and waved to the audience.

Finn noticed Mr. Labanzo standing next to Principal Biggs in the back of the auditorium.

"The only student who can perform that trick in my class . . . is Finn," Mr. Labanzo said. "I'm amazed. Is that really Felix?"

Finn watched as Mr. Click, the computer-lab teacher, entered the rear of the auditorium. He walked directly over to Principal Biggs and started talking to him.

Finn bowed again as the audience remained standing and cheering. As he looked up, he saw Mr. Labanzo and the principal walking down the aisle toward the stage. Finn knew instantly what was going to happen if he stayed. If they looked at him closely, his secret would be out. But he had planned for this.

Finn quickly leaned toward Liddy and explained to her what to do. He then sat down in the chair.

Liddy pulled the curtain in front of him as he continued to wave.

After counting to three, she pulled it back.

The applause grew louder.

Finn had vanished.

CHAPTER ELEVEN

Principal Biggs and Mr. Labanzo climbed the stairs to the stage. The principal walked to the center.

"I never knew how many talented students we have," Principal Biggs said. "I want to thank all of them for performing today. The awards will be announced in ten minutes."

The trapdoor in the stage floor had worked. Finn had dropped down into a small room underneath the stage with the help of the stage crew. He then used a corridor underneath the stage to reach an exit door located offstage.

When the principal and Mr. Labanzo walked into the dressing room, Finn stood up. He had just finished putting Felix's costume away.

"Finn, we didn't expect to see you back-stage," Principal Biggs said.

Finn quickly pushed Felix's bag away from him. He smiled as the sweat ran down his forehead. There was a lingering red mark around his eyes where the mask had been.

"Have you seen Felix around here?" Principal Biggs asked.

"No," Finn replied. Finn could feel a nervous twitch go through his body.

"If you see him, let him know the principal and Mr. Labanzo would like to talk to him," said Principal Biggs.

"I heard you did a great job on the spotlight for the dance group," Mr. Labanzo said.

"Thanks," replied Finn.

Mr. Labanzo looked carefully at Finn and lowered his voice. "And something tells me Felix should be thanking you for his magic performance."

Principal Biggs and Mr. Labanzo left the dressing room. Finn felt the nervous twitch go away.

Finn now needed to find Botts. He wiped the sweat off his face and left the dressing room. He found Botts cleaning his unicycle in one of the backstage rooms. Chocolate frosting was on the tires and spokes. There was also a big ring of chocolate frosting around Botts's mouth.

"You didn't tell me Taz was part of your act," Finn said, standing in the doorway.

"I didn't know either until he decided to crash it," Botts replied angrily. "Would I ever agree to someone throwing a perfectly good chocolate donut at me?"

"Given the fact that you go to Aunt Z's Bakery almost every week for a chocolate donut, I would say no," Finn said, laughing.

"Have you told the principal about Taz?" Finn asked.

"Yes," Botts replied. "He's looking for him right now."

Finn looked outside the doorway toward the dressing rooms.

"And there he is," Finn said. "And Felix and Gator are with him."

CHAPTER TWELVE

Felix, Taz, and Gator walked down the hallway past the dressing rooms and onto the backstage area. Felix wandered over to where Ringo and the rest of his band were standing. Finn watched Felix as he laughed and talked with Ringo. Finn wondered how sick Felix really was.

Suddenly the voice of Principal Biggs filled the auditorium. Finn and Botts walked onto the stage behind the curtains, just outside of view from the audience. Principal Biggs was standing in the middle of the stage.

"Thank you for waiting," Principal Biggs said. "Before I announce the awards, I need to let you know that effective immediately, the computer lab will be closed while we make changes to the network. Someone gained access to the school's computer system this afternoon and made grade changes. If you have any information about who might have done this, please let me know immediately."

The audience went silent.

Awards were given to two groups. The first group was made up of students who sang, danced, or played an instrument. The second group was everyone else. Principal Biggs began with the awards for the first group. He awarded third place to Selina, Tara, Elle, and Willow for their dance performance. Second place went to Veronica for her song. And first place was awarded to Tess. Tess was giving students high fives as she walked down the

aisle toward the stage. With a big smile on her face, she accepted the first-place trophy from Principal Biggs.

"Due to the overwhelming response," Principal Biggs said, "I've decided to create a new category. The award for best comedy performance goes to . . . Botts."

Students clapped and cheered. Botts twitched his nose and shrugged, then walked onto the stage.

"Is Taz here?" Principal Biggs asked.

Botts pointed to the back of the stage.

"Taz, please come out," Principal Biggs said.

Taz was in shock as he walked onto the stage. Principal Biggs shook Botts's hand. The audience applauded.

Principal Biggs stepped away from the microphone and confronted Taz.

"I've been told your performance with Botts was not planned," Principal Biggs said sternly.

Taz said nothing.

"I would like to talk to you afterward."

The principal then returned to the microphone and began the award presentations for the second group. He awarded the third-place trophy to Yang and Zhang for their kung fu performance and second place to the pogo-stick jumper.

"I now wish to announce the winner for the first-place trophy," Principal Biggs said. "Our judges were unanimous in this choice. And the first-place trophy goes to . . . Felix."

Felix's jaw dropped. The audience cheered wildly. Felix walked past Finn.

"You get the performance, I get the trophy," Felix said quietly. "Seems like a fair trade to me."

Finn stared back without responding. Felix walked onto the stage and stood next to Principal Biggs.

"Congratulations, Felix," said the principal.

Mr. Labanzo walked onto the stage from the opposite side and whispered something to the principal.

"Felix," Principal Biggs said, "remind us what your trick was called."

Felix suddenly went pale and looked around for Finn. Finn hid behind a backstage curtain.

"Ummmm . . . that trick . . . that trick is called . . . the magic-box trick," Felix stammered.

"And that's the one you performed today?" the principal asked.

"Ummmm . . . yes," Felix answered.

The audience began to whisper.

"And what part of that trick did you like the most?" Principal Biggs asked.

"When I made the plant and animals come to life," Felix said. His voice sounded desperate.

Someone started to boo.

"Did you use a chair as part of your performance?" the principal asked.

"No . . . maybe . . . ." Felix replied. He could no longer hide the panicked look on his face.

Principal Biggs and Felix immediately walked off the stage. Mr. Labanzo followed. The principal motioned to Taz and Gator to follow him.

The principal, Mr. Labanzo, and Mr. Click—with his three computer grade printouts—went into a backstage room with Felix, Taz, and Gator. The door was closed. Finn and Botts could see Principal Biggs talking with all the boys through a glass window. In less than a minute, he came out and walked back onto the stage.

"I apologize for the delay," Principal Biggs said. "But I need to change the winner of our first-place trophy. For reasons I will announce tomorrow, Felix did not perform in today's talent show. It appears we have a very talented student who performed a very impressive magic trick in Felix's place and is much more deserving. I'm pleased to announce that the first-place trophy goes to Finn."

Finn struggled to breathe. His heart pounded. This was the last thing he expected.

With some hesitation, Finn walked onto the stage. There was instant applause as Finn reached center stage. All the students, parents, and teachers were on their feet. The applause continued, and the students now chanted, "Finn! Finn! Finn!"

Principal Biggs handed the trophy to Finn. He turned to the audience and waved.

"Congratulations," Principal Biggs said. "True talent can't hide."

. . .

The next morning at the end of school, Principal Biggs announced that Felix, Taz, and Gator had gained access to the school computer system. They had been responsible for making grade changes to their student records, as well as many others'. Mr. Click received an alert on his computer when the changes were made.

Felix had planned on using Finn as an alibi. If questioned, Felix would say he performed at the talent show as scheduled. Felix had not planned on winning a trophy. Taz, realizing he had missed his spot in the talent show, had simply come up with the idea to join Botts during his performance as another unicycle rider. Gator had been too confident that no one would miss him.

Finn and Botts exited the front doors of the school following the last bell.

"Botts," Finn said, "stop your whining about winning a trophy."

"Easy for you to say," Botts replied. "It cost me two boxes of chocolate donuts."

"Finn!" a voice interrupted them from behind.

Finn turned around. It was Liddy. She ran up to them.

"I was wondering if I could be your assistant for your next magic act," she said. "I think we all know now that the real magician with the initials *FF* is you, Finn Fasser."

"Sure," Finn said in shock. This was the last thing he expected to hear from Liddy. "Botts was ready to quit anyway."

"Your parents would have been really proud of you today," Liddy added. "See you around." She turned and walked back to the school.

"Wow, a trophy and a new assistant," Botts said. "How about using some of your magic to get me two more boxes of chocolate donuts?"

"I'll have to work on that trick," Finn said. "But I owe you for getting my bag. Would you settle for one donut at Aunt Z's?"

ABOUT THE AUTHOR

Stew Knight is the author of the Finn & Botts chapter book series. Despite being one of the most avid readers and attentive students in his second-grade class, he would still find it funny to yell at random moments to disrupt his teacher if she was being too boring—a stunt that his teacher didn't let slide without discipline. But the discipline worked, because Knight's imagination developed to the point where nothing was ever boring again. He thanks his second-grade teacher for helping his imagination grow enough to become an author.

Knight lives in Salt Lake City, Utah, with his wife and very anxious poodle. He enjoys the outdoors and can be found on the ski slopes in the winter, hiking the Wasatch Range of the Rocky Mountains in the spring and summer, and hanging out with the pigs at the annual state fair in the fall.

DISCARD

CPSIA information can be obtained
at www.ICGtesting.com
Printed in the USA
LVHW111418251020
669761LV00004B/1061